Heman Rowlee Timlow

In Memoriam

Heman Rowlee Timlow

In Memoriam

ISBN/EAN: 9783337375652

Printed in Europe, USA, Canada, Australia, Japan

Cover: Foto ©Andreas Hilbeck / pixelio.de

More available books at **www.hansebooks.com**

𝔍𝔫 𝔐𝔢𝔪𝔬𝔯𝔦𝔞𝔪

Died—At Rhinebeck, October 5, 1866, ELIZABETH PLATT, beloved wife of CHARLES H. ADAMS of Cohoes, and daughter of WILLIAM B. PLATT of Rhinebeck, in the 37th year of her age.

NEW YORK

BRADSTREET PRESS

1867

BRIGHTON HEIGHTS, S. I.,

Feb. 1st, 1867.

To CHARLES H. ADAMS, Esq.:

It is fitting that your name should introduce these pages, memorial of your sainted wife. This tribute to womanly nobleness and piety has been a work of love. Its imperfections none feel more than myself. The record is now before the public, and underneath the imperfect vestment a human hand has wrought, will be clearly discerned the lustre of a character worthy of exact imitation.

To the care and consolations of the wise and loving Father I would commend your wounded spirit, and the dear children who nevermore on earth will know a mother's sweet caress and counsel.

Very truly your friend,

HEMAN R. TIMLOW.

I.

" In whose hand thy breath is."—DANIEL, v. 23.

" My times are in thy hands."—PSALMS, XXXI. 15.

" It matters not how long we live, but how."—FESTUS.

" He most lives
Who thinks most, feels the noblest, acts the best ;
And he whose heart beats quickest lives the longest—
Lives in one hour more than in years do some."—FESTUS.

An ancient philosopher died at ninety. The thought of his approaching end had for some time disturbed him. He could not be reconciled to the fact. His past experience, he felt, had but prepared him to live in the world he was so soon to leave. The pleasing delusion was indulged, that just in sight was the

1

2

summit of Human Knowledge and Happiness. The heart desired no greater good than to stand on that proud height. All
was gladness and exultation at the bright prospect. But the philosopher's vision vanished; his hopes perished. The sands beneath his feet began to give way, and he sank back, he could not
tell whither.

Like this venerable teacher of antiquity, many now mistake the
design and limitations of the present state of being. Too often
is it assumed to be complete in itself. The mass of mankind
spend their energies upon transient objects as upon an ultimate
end. And yet who does not know that the reach of vision is so
narrow, the subjects of inquiry extend to relations so far beyond
our power to trace them, that only imperfect and unsatisfactory
conclusions can be attained? The future is concealed by a curtain impenetrable to mortal vision, and which no mortal power

can draw aside. Independent of that Revelation that brought Life and Immortality to light, no knowledge is possible concerning those things after which the mind most anxiously asks. When, then, those not having this Revelation, or, having it, neglect and depart from its instructions, attempt to decide upon the wisdom of conditions affecting this life, they must always err. That Eye which ranges over the Universe of Matter and Spirit, and that Infinite Mind which planned "from of old" the operations of Law and Intelligence, looks and orders far beyond where a creature can follow. "Who by searching can find out God?"

It has been well said, that every life on earth is a plan of God. No one liveth, however briefly, who is not linked to purposes that run out into and through eternity. A death is sometimes pronounced untimely. So we speak when the young and the strong pass away, or when any are slain by accident. Who has not stood dumb at the bier of those cut down by the Destroyer

in the meridian of their days? The mind is bewildered and har-

assed at the spectacle of a life that seems to have been but half

finished. But do any depart from the world "out of season?"

Nay! We are taught that God has put bounds to every life.

His own hand marks out every path. In Divine Wisdom are

the years of every man told. Old and young are subject to the

same law of mortality God has wisely established, but the peculiar

principles and methods of this law have never been disclosed.

The "little ones" even, who come

"As living shadows for a moment seen,"

and tarry only to plant new affections in the yearning parent's

heart, and then wing their way "to bright worlds beyond," are no

less charged with a mission on earth than they of three-score and

ten. We know not this mission. The life thus bounded by a

moment seems a vain thing. Our eyes looked upon a bud, but God's eye saw both blossom and fruit. God set the germ, and the plant grew and bore fruit, ere we knew that ray or dew had fallen upon it.

Life is not measured by length of days; nor can it be measured by man at all. When it should end, none dare decide. Who is there so bold as to even wish to know? The wish and wisdom of man are but mockery of the purposes of Him whose "ways are past finding out." Had the shadow gone back on the dial of the philosopher, and another century been leased him, that summit for which his heart panted could never have felt his weary feet. The vision might have tarried, but never have been realized. This is the theater of preparation for something better, something higher. Children are we all, burdened with a child's perplexities, vagaries, follies, and yet glowing with precious prophecies, and laden with types as pledges of the future. The perfect stature, the fruition of promise and hope, lie beyond.

When Mirza mourned the vanity and misery and mortality of his race, as these had been presented to him in vision, the Genius that had been charged with his care compassionated his sorrow, and called him from the sad sight. "Look no more," said his spirit-companion, "on man in the first stage of his existence, in his setting out for eternity, but cast thine eye on that thick mist into which the tide bears the several generations of mortals that fall into it." Mirza looked, and the mist had vanished. Spread before his entranced eye was a scene surpassing in loveliness what the boldest imagination had ventured. He was now content, if from a state so full of trial and suffering, and strangely unequal condition, it were possible to ascend to such glory.

What is here a fable becomes real to every eye of faith that turns from the disappointments and woes and universal unrest to which this world gives birth, and pierces the cloud that hides the Better Land. There, every thing is uncovered : hidden purposes are revealed; painful experiences are all explained; the old learn why they so long lived; the young have disclosed why they so early were transplanted. In clear light shall be read the hidden things of birth, life, death, and all that now we know not. Then, as not now, shall we be impressed and made glad as we turn to the Father and say, " My times are in thy hands." As we so well know the plans of God in this world, let us abide in His wisdom. Let not the heart grow faint, nor the hands weary in His service. "All the days of my appointed time will I wait, till my change come." " So teach us to number our days that we may apply our hearts unto wisdom."

II.

"A virtuous woman is a crown to her husband."—PROV., XII. 4.

"There shall also this, that this woman hath done, be told for a memorial of her."—MATT., XXVI. 13.

"The idea of her life shall sweetly creep
Into his study of imagination,
And every lovely organ of her life
Shall come appareled in more precious habit,
More moving delicate, and full of life,
Into the eye and prospect of his soul,
Than when she lived indeed."—SHAKSPEARE.

It is a providence not easily interpreted that has removed ELIZABETH PLATT ADAMS from friends, and home, and church on earth. There is much connected with her life, her sufferings, her death, that we vainly attempt to understand. Had

2

we not the belief that Infinite Wisdom and Love have presided in her history as in all else, cheerless and dark would be every thought her name awakens. "Shall not the Judge of all the earth do right?" The Lord appoints "a time to be born" and "a time to die." "The Lord gave, the Lord hath taken away; blessed be the name of the Lord."

Blessed memories cluster about the name of Mrs. Adams. Those who knew her from birth, and followed her with watchful and affectionate interest till the grave hid her from human view, are pained by no recollection. Not that perfection was hers. No one would disclaim it more sincerely and vehemently than she. But with whatever of weakness, there was an absence of willfulness, which too often mars the character, and incurs indifference, if not enmity. What of faults there were lingered not long in the memory. The bright light shed all about by the superior qualities of mind and heart too strongly drew the gaze of observers, to admit to prominence those natural infirmities to which all are heir. It is not, then, the perfection of excellence that these pages propose to exhibit, but a beautiful pattern, reflecting much of Him whom we worship as Infinite Perfection.

The discoverer of the Hudson River pronounced it the most beautiful river in the world, and the praise he bestowed has been perpetuated in story and song. No one sails up the noble stream without an awakened enthusiasm akin to that of the people who first settled upon its banks. It is still what it always was; its beauties are none diminished, although its shores more and more "glow with the colors of civilization." It was on the banks of this river that Margaret Fuller felt herself "enfranchised in the society of Nature." Others, like her, have been lost in contemplating the majesty of scenery furnished by these splendid creations of Divine Art.

It was the pride of Mrs. Adams, that amid these grand scenes she had her birth. No heart kindled into greater enthusiasm when in the presence of the river, with its bluffs and mountains swelling up on either side. She often remarked the tranquil pleasure she took in recalling these to mind, when separated from them. Distance nor absence ever chilled the affection of her heart for her native scenery.

She was born in Rhinebeck, N. Y., February 6th, 1830. Her parents were William B. and Sarah Stoutenburgh Platt. Religious influences surrounded her from the time she could receive the first impression. No child was ever more carefully and tenderly reared. As the only daughter, she lacked no attention that fond parents could minister. But the indulgence she received at home did not develop the spirit of selfishness, as is often the case. There was a natural softness, grace and ease of character, which were not affected by the partial and lavish attention bestowed upon her. And it must greatly comfort the father and mother in their present sorrow, that their unwearied care was ever met by the most comely respect and tender love. Her duty as a daughter she faithfully discharged. As a sister, she still lives in the heart of one who bears in constant remembrance the mild radiance she cast over his childhood days, and the sweet sympathy that bound her to him in his riper years.

At school and in the social life of her native village, she won affection as at home. From teachers and companions, there comes but one testimony. In the class she was dutiful and prompt. Among her mates she knew not distinctions, but sustained friendly intercourse with all. She had a kind word for those in trouble, and "wept with those that weep." Thus, with even and consistent life, she passed her childhood and youth. Although not averse to gayety, no one ever accused her of thoughtlessness. Although not yet moulded by the Spirit of Christ into His likeness, she was by no means irreligious. She was loyal to her convictions of right and truth, and failed not in outward duties.

It is uncertain when really began her true spiritual life. Her guilelessness and moral propriety some would identify with her religious life, and thus pronounce her always a child of God. But she was not satisfied with her earlier conduct and experiences. There was yet a distance from God. Not yet had she drawn so close to her Saviour as to feel the warmth of His presence. She longed for a nearness to Him, even for a resting-place on His bosom, where she might lean and feel the beatings of His loving heart.

This blessed state she reached in the autumn of eighteen hundred and fifty-two. For several months, her mind had been more directly given to religious meditation. While she could not reproach herself with want of love for earthly kindred and friends, she felt convicted of not giving God the supreme place in her heart. His claims she now saw as never before. Her neglect of these, and His long-suffering and forbearance, His pleading mercy and free grace, moved her to profound repentance. In deep humility, she cast herself at her Father's feet, and through the Lord Jesus, sought and found full forgiveness. Her peculiar experiences at this time are not fully known. If she recorded them, the record has not been seen by other than herself. To her pastor, she gave satisfactory evidence of a great change wrought within. As to the matter of a public confession, she had many struggles. At last she was enabled to discern clearly the path of duty. Conversing with her mother upon the subject, she said: "*My mind is made up.*" This expression may be taken as a key to her conduct. She deliberately formed her judgment and abided by the decision. In August, eighteen hundred and fifty-two, she united with the Reformed Dutch Church, Rhinebeck, N. Y., then under the pastoral care of Rev. Peter Stryker, D.D., now of the Thirty-fourth Street Reformed Dutch Church, New York City. From that time till her death, she was a consistent and growing Christian.

In September of this same year, she was married to Charles H. Adams, Esq., of Cohoes, N. Y. This marriage was

fruitful of the utmost happiness. But now she was introduced to a new class of temptations, and which would
thoroughly sift her Christian character. There was hardly
anything that her position could not command. Every desire for bodily comfort or pleasure could be promptly met.
She had access to the best society. She was beset by those
influences that too often overcome the heart and indulge
gross selfishness. But no one could discover that these in
the least unfavorably affected her. She was just as unselfish,
free from pride, as simple-hearted, as devout, as ever. Her
life, in these respects, is a rebuke to those who, from high
social positions, look haughtily upon the poor, and who
employ every art to maintain association with the rich, fash-
ionable and gay. Mrs. Adams looked with contempt on
the formality and show that distinguish much of American

society. Her heart was formed for sincere and not formal friendships; hence her abhorrence of social deceits. She freely mingled with the poor, and had that most desirable of all traits, when among them, of so conducting as never to remind them of their poverty. Her conversation and charities flowed from a heart so tender and simple, that the objects of her benevolence were never made uneasy or unhappy in receiving gifts. Her last pastor, the Rev. Dr. Waldron, writes of the mourning her death occasioned among the poor of Cohoes, "to whom she gave not only of the abundance with which God had blessed her, but whose homes she so often visited, and whose hearts she comforted with kindly words of sympathy." In this respect, she may be commended as a beautiful example of that "pure religion and undefiled before God and the Father" which "is this: to visit the fatherless and widows in their affliction, and to keep himself unspotted from the world."

She loved the sanctuary and the place of prayer. When ill-health did not interpose, her place was filled. Not as a matter of custom or form did she enter the courts of the Lord, but for praise and worship. No small measure of the Psalmist's spirit was hers, and with him she could devoutly say : " A day in thy courts is better than a thousand. I had rather be a door-keeper in the house of my God than to dwell in the tents of wickedness." Her religion was of a type to make her happy. She could not reconcile gloominess and a true Christian faith. It will be remembered by all who knew her, how rarely there was other than pleasant expression and tone of voice. " She was remarkable for her Christian cheerfulness," writes Dr. Waldron, "and trustfulness of character; ever disposed to look on the bright side, and to encourage the troubled and desponding. We shall miss her pleasant countenance in the place of prayer, and regret that her praises on earth are hushed in silence."

The religion she professed exhibited its power in every relation of life. As a wife, mother, daughter and sister, she felt herself indebted to this power. Although naturally lovely and affectionate, her piety added a charm none could resist; it led her to think less of worldly estate and interests, and to have chief solicitude about the spiritual. With the writer she held frequent conversations, in which her near friends were subjects, and he does not remember a single instance where success in this life appeared to be an object of concern, but with much and anxious solicitude she spoke of their spiritual condition. She longed for the time when all her loved ones could, with her, sit at the table of the Lord. While this desire was not gratified on earth, will not the living so prepare themselves, that they may hereafter have a place with her at the Marriage Supper of the Lamb?

There is a sacredness about the home circle we are forbidden to invade. How much she loved, and how much she was loved, words are too poor to tell; we dare not trust the pen to attempt an expression. How dear she was to husband and children, it is not ours to measure, but it is theirs to feel, as the affectionate impulses of the heart go out vainly after her, now removed from the sight. She lingers with parents and brother as a dream of sweetest import, and yet so real, that a dark, lonely void exists which naught else but reunion can supply. She had a deep place in many hearts, and none knew her but to mourn when she "fell asleep."

III.

"Thou in faithfulness hast afflicted me."—PSALM, CXIX. 75.

"When he hath tried me, I shall come forth as gold."—JOB, XXIII. 10.

"The best of men
That ere wore earth about him was a sufferer,
A soft, meek, patient, humble, tranquil spirit."—DECKER.

The instances are few where every comfort for body and soul could be so readily commanded as by Mrs. Adams. Truer, more affectionate and self-denying friends, none could wish. Every physical and social indulgence, every gratification of the taste and feelings, had at hand ample means for any supply. Were it possible for outward condition to furnish grounds for complete enjoyment of this life, this surely had been her inheritance. But her life, especially her latter years, had its experience of bitterness. She was a sufferer. In early life, the frailness of her constitution was not so apparent. Yet there were indications of physical weakness that led friends to be solicitous about the future. Occasionally very ill, yet her nearest friends were not really alarmed until a few months before her decease. Her difficulties were complicated, and some doubts prevailed as to their precise nature. The best skill of the earthly physician was baffled, in treating the disorder. It numbered another, and the fairest too, among its myriad victims. Her final sickness was somewhat protracted, and at times very painful. But every suffering was endured patiently. She neither murmured nor rebelled against the Providence that afflicted her. As far as possible she concealed her sufferings, lest her friends might be pained.

In the closing month of the Spring, she was brought from New York, where she had spent many weary weeks upon her bed, to her father's house at Rhinebeck. It was at this time the writer was first persuaded of her sure and rapid decline. Visiting her, he felt it a duty to discover, if possible, her convictions with reference to herself. Scarcely was the subject of her sickness alluded to, before she unhesitatingly and without emotion remarked that she felt this to be her last sickness. Her conversation turned upon the attractions the world had for her. She spoke of her husband and children, how very precious they were. The affection and kindness other friends lavished upon her were noticed. But she felt, that her afflictions had been qualifying her for something better than this world could furnish. Dear as were friends, delightful as were the associations and privileges of life, these must all be surrendered to the will of her Father, whom she knew did not "afflict willingly." Her prayer was, that she might be submissive. For this she earnestly struggled. Those who watched over or who occasionally visited her during the last three months of her life, could not but remark a wonderful passiveness. Week after week she lay like a child in her Father's arms, exhibiting the spirit expressed by the words, "Even so, Father, for so it seemed good in thy sight." A friend, who knew much of her inner life and struggles, has said, that for months, while persuaded that remedies were useless, she yet would willingly take any remedy proposed by anxious friends for her relief, in order to gratify them in their desire to exhaust every possible resource. She would add to her own sufferings, to preserve them in hope or diminish their sorrows. So unselfish was she, that she labored to suppress sighs and groans, lest some loving heart might be wounded as they were heard. This tenderness for others did not at all abate; until the last she was forgetful of self. Her afflictions had wrought a good work, in that now she was complete victor. Indeed, her prayer had been to have the cup pass if possible, yet the high attainment was made— *Not my will, but thine, O God! be done.*

The Captain of our salvation was made perfect through sufferings. The same discipline of sorrow He adopts to perfect His people. He led His handmaid into a furnace, and she went up therefrom as gold tried and purified.

IV.

It is related that, as a visitor to the Escurial stood gazing
on Titian's celebrated painting of the Last Supper, he was
accosted by an old hermit of St. Jerome, and addressed as
follows: "I have sat in sight of that picture for nearly three-
score years. During that time, my companions have dropped

off one after another; all who were my seniors, all who were my cotemporaries, and many or most of those who were younger than myself. More than one generation has passed away, and there the figures in the picture have remained unchanged. I look at these, till I sometimes think they are the realities, and we but the shadows."

There is an unbroken procession of generations to the grave, but the places that knew them remain. The mountains and hills and water-courses, the sun, moon and stars, pass not away. Who is not often impressed, as was the hermit, with the fugitive and shadowy features of human life, and who is not at times disposed to indulge suspicions that change is more an attribute of life than of inanimate matter? We revisit the place of nativity after years of absence. We gaze on an unchanged face of Nature. The

same venerable forests are there. We are sheltered by familiar trees. Through the same valleys we roam, and plant
the feet on rocks whose mossy surface invited the gentler
frolics of childhood. The noise of the waterfall and the
voice of bird, vary not a note from olden time, and now
discourse a music more entrancing than the delicate instru-
ment of strings. Even the old habitations are there. And
yet how vainly we look for forms and faces who went to
and fro in our early days! The one indeed seem the realities; the other but the shadows.

But such is life. "Man that is born of a woman is of
few days and full of trouble." "He cometh forth like a
flower, and is cut down: he fleeth also as a shadow, and
continueth not." "We all do fade as the leaf." "Our
days upon earth are a shadow." All this is abundantly

verified by daily experience. In the morning, at mid-day, the sun goes down. The young, the beautiful, the good, as a vapor, vanish away.

So passed from earth, ELIZABETH PLATT ADAMS. Her native mountains still endure, as they ever have, while repeated generations have departed. But we know that she is deathless, while they shall yet be consumed. Deathless indeed!—and yet dead!

The decline of Mrs. Adams was rapid. During the summer, she frequently rode in her carriage; but as autumn came on, her weakness increased, and she soon was confined to the house. She was perfectly aware of her decline, and had given up all hope of recovery; but she did not communicate her belief to her family. On Sunday, August fifth, she was visited by the writer. He had been for some weeks absent from

Rhinebeck, on a vacation, and in the mean time had received a call to another field. As he entered the room, Mrs. Adams was very much affected, and after a few moments remarked: "I hoped that you would not leave here, until I had gone."

"Do you feel that you are so near the Better Land?"

"I *know* I am almost there."

"Are you willing and ready?"

"I feel that I am."

"Have you had many struggles of mind, in view of your separation from all you hold dear in the world?"

"Oh! yes. It seems to me sometimes that I have more to live for than most persons. I have the kindest of husbands; my children are a great comfort to me; all the family are very near; and there is nothing that I wish for that I cannot have. The world seems very pleasant to me, and if it were God's will, I would like to live longer. But I know I can live but a short time. I try to be submissive and patient; I pray to be so. I desired very much to be at the Communion to-day. I expected ———— to unite with the Church to-day; but he is so timid. If he and ———— and ———— were true Christians, how happy we would all be! To-day I have prayed for them all."

"You have no doubts and fears to trouble you now?"

"No! I rest on Jesus. I can do nothing; He will do all."

"Then, all is peace?"

"Yes: Peace! Peace!" After a short pause she said: "I hope that it will not be so that you cannot be at my funeral." As she desired, so it was.

A few weeks later, the writer saw her again. Her faith

and hope were none diminished. The interview was in presence of her husband and mother. She spoke freely and confidently, but yet in a most touching tone and with deep emotion, added : "It would be pleasant for me to live." It seemed that as the end drew near, her family became increasedly precious, and sometimes, in the weakness of the body, but not of faith, would she express a desire to remain with them. At no interview, however, did she indicate a want of submission to the will of God.

Her sufferings gradually increased. To her most hopeful friends, her case now became hopeless. The end drew near. The last week of September was one of great anxiety to her friends. She rallied again, however. On the morning of October fourth, appeared unmistakable evidences of a speedy release from her sufferings. Her physician was almost constantly with her, and his presence gave her much comfort in view of the approaching struggle.

In the afternoon, she summoned the household, servants and all, to her bedside. To the servants, she spake kindly words, and bade them all good-by. The heart-stricken parents received the last loving words and kiss from the loving daughter. Her two little ones she embraced, and gave to them affectionate counsels. In true faith, she committed them to the care of Him who hears the faithful mother's prayer, and regards her faith long after she is dead. Sweet words were they she spake to him who was to her more than all the world besides. His head was bowed in heavy grief; his heart was wrung with agony, as he felt that "part of very self" was being torn from him. But those last whispers of love, the affectionate imprint, the prayer, the meek surrender to the Father, the victory of grace, lifted the head and soothed the heart. Could he but rejoice in Him, who giveth such a victory? The Lord stood by, mingling gladness with that cup of sorrow. He gave to the smitten husband " beauty for ashes, the oil of joy for mourning, the garment of praise for the spirit of heaviness."

The stream of life had narrowed and shallowed until all ran in a little rill. Energy had wasted, until all activity blended solely in desire—simple breathing after submission and conformity to the Lord's will. Too much worn out now for thinking, the mind thus sublimely withdraws into another realm — " I am done with earth and earthly things. Come, Lord Jesus, come quickly!"

She died at a time when probably she would have chosen, had her wish been consulted; and no day was more con-

genial to her tastes than that in which she was carried to the
sanctuary of the dead.   She loved October and October
scenes.   She left the earth clothed as she most admired:
the chill had strewn the ground with drooping plants; the
frosts impearled every blade and branch, and the morning sun
spread the verdant earth as with a covering of diamonds.
The last fragrance of the flower had disappeared on the wings
of the autumn winds.   The sun never set where his beams
lit up with more splendor earth and sky, than on that last
day she spent below.   Such evening glory we not often behold.   There seemed to be a sympathy of Nature with the
setting sun of that beautiful life.   There followed an hour
of darkness ere release came; but it only was a symbol of
the brief darkness of death—an hour when the spirit is strug-
gling to disenthrall itself, and enter upon its rest.

The day of burial came. The hills about, "from base to crest," were veiled in that mellow haze which in autumn often rests on the region of the Catskills. The air was soft and balmy, stirred only by the gentlest breezes. How much she who was to be borne hence loved such a day, they know, who remember with what glowing but unconscious enthusiasm she went forth, in ride or walk, to enjoy it. But now the eye was dimmed, and saw not the calm glory it so often traced. Other eyes saw and kindred spirits spoke, in her name, of the tranquil beauties of the sky and the richly robed hills and fields. It was a sad day for friends; yet they could not but be grateful that her bondage of suffering was broken. They gathered in solemn assembly. From far and near they came; from the high circles in which she had moved in modest dignity, and from among the poor who had received her generous benefactions, came many to shed tears of

profound sorrow at her grave. It was no affectation of grief

that distinguished the company of mourners the occasion

called together. It was a time of deep solemnity. Every

heart was full, and spoke through an eloquent silence. The

scene was one of simplicity. The absence of art and form

made it sublime. The coffin, the flowers, only less fragrant

than her deeds of charity, the order of the obsequies, were in

accord with simple, unaffected grief. A few familiar sentences,

the lessons of Scripture, and a prayer introduced the services.

Afterward, an address was made by him whom herself weeks

before had desired to officiate. In obedience to request, it is

here given :

Address.

"Sad, sad indeed the event that calls us together at this time. To this hour have anxious hearts long looked. Amid the exciting alternations of hope and fear, have tender hands ministered to the pressing needs of her whose death we so deeply deplore. If the consuming desire of husband and children and parents and brother had been consulted or availed, this chilled form had now been instinct and warm with life; the flush of health would light up these sunken cheeks, and from these sealed lips would flow, as in other days, sweet words to delight and bless this bereaved circle of love. But the Destroying Angel heeded not the prayers agonized hearts put up for her deliverance. Vainly had the best medical skill and care of friends been bestowed to prevent this sore bereavement.

6

The fondest hopes have perished ; the tenderest ties that bind the heart on earth, have been sundered. Hard is it to confess the dreadful reality! But, alas! it is too true!

"Gladly would I have been spared this hour. Personally, believe me, I am distressed at this providence. It is a painful fact to me that my last service to this people should be as it is. And yet, since such a service has been allotted, there is much in the attending circumstances to comfort the heart.

"With gratitude may we think of the sister gone, as a disciple, a *true* disciple of the Lord Jesus Christ. More than thirteen years since, she surrendered her heart to God. After many and severe struggles, she determined to make a public profession of her faith. This she did in August, eighteen hundred and fifty-three. Since that time, her life has been so consistent, that I believe no one ever questioned her attainments in holiness. Her piety was without mixture of that ostentation that too often mars the Christian profession. God had surrounded her with all that could command social position and almost every bodily gratification. Yet her wealth was never appropriated to nourish vanity; no position in life could persuade her to assume superiority over the lowliest fellow-disciple; no flattery could succeed in raising selfishness to supremacy; nothing in look, word, or act betrayed a thought offensive to any with whom she came in contact. It is rare, in this imperfect world, to see one so beautiful, so gifted with traits commanding universal admiration and respect, so bountifully supplied with worldly goods, who to the same degree is free from pride, selfishness and show. This I say, not in the spirit of eulogy, but to commend an example you all confess to be of great beauty and power. To natural loveliness were added "gifts and graces" the Divine Spirit only confers. The heart had been melted into submission and freely given to the Father. Her Christian life was so even and distinguished for so much of simplicity, as to furnish but few of those striking particulars found in many current biographies. All who knew her marked her guilelessness, trustful spirit, hopefulness, love of the unseen Saviour, and sincere obedience. Be ye all followers of her as she followed Christ.

"To the end, her faith endured. Months ago, she was satisfied that the end was not far off. Lest she might pain her friends, she abstained from allusion to the fact. Near the close of life, this silence was broken.

"It was on Friday last, when, assured of the nearness of her departure, she, in childlike faith, bade adieu to this world.

To the sorrowing household, she gave parting counsels and greetings and kisses. After an affecting interview with her husband, she said to him, 'I am done with earth and earthly things;' then folding the hands, sweetly breathed the prayer: 'Come, Lord Jesus, come quickly!' Not long after, the Saviour came and took her to His arms.

"I shall not, in this presence, enter her home, to draw from thence facts to exhibit her virtues or impress her personal worth upon you. The life connected with her family relations, is the treasure of this smitten husband, these motherless children, these crushed parents, and of the absent one, who as yet knows not his bitter sorrow. It must mitigate much the keenness of grief, on this occasion, to feel that *such* a wife, mother, daughter, sister, friend, is taken. Pleasant and comforting in future days will be the recollection of her excellent name. How fragrant her memory! What a legacy to these children, her virtues, as in after life they will hear them told! Bright will be their path, if they walk in her steps.

"But vain are such consolations, when alone our dependence. I would fail in my trust did I not point you to the promises and hopes and Grace revealed in the Gospel. God hath done it; He doeth all things well. This providence is wise, although now not so discerned; it is sent in love, although heavy the stroke. The Lord hath said: 'What I do ye know not now, but shall know hereafter.' Trust in the Father's Love and Wisdom, and take to yourselves the assurances of the Gospel. She has but gone before, and there will await your coming. Not far off is the hour of re-union. Through the same Saviour, you may ascend to her.

"Oh! lift the eye above, and let faith unveil the invisible

world.   Her crown is cast at the Saviour's feet.   Her voice

is chanting anthems with the Heavenly Choir.   No pains rack

the body there ; no tear fills the eye; no sorrow touches the

heart.   From that pavilion of glory, she sends back to you

the most affectionate pleading, to be prepared to have a fel-

lowship with her in that happy land ; to make sure of your

inheritance among the saints of God; to press toward the mark

for the prize of the high calling of God in Christ Jesus.

" My brother, your sorrow is the great sorrow of life.

Would that I had the power to fill your heart with the com-

fort you need.   But neither myself nor this tearful and sym-

pathizing assembly can do it.   But there is One who can

do all you wish and need—the same Father who has taken

your dear wife.   By His Grace, the union begun, and con-

tinued thirteen years on earth, may be perfected among the stars. There, no rude hand can sever the tie. Here, all is transient ; there, enduring evermore. Hope then, that your hearts and voices shall yet blend in the delightful interchanges and praises of the Heavenly Home. Not long hence will you and these dear children, and these broken-hearted parents, and the loved one now out upon the great sea, and ourselves who mingle tears with yours, be selected at the Marriage Supper of the Lamb.

"To you all, gathered here to-day, I would speak as for the last time, to warn you to be prepared for such an event as this. There are voices streaming from this coffin more impressive than the voice of the living preacher, and they solemnly remind you of the brevity of life, the certainty and nearness of death, and the important duty of preparing to exchange worlds. Oh ! listen not vainly to these voices !

Heed, oh! heed them! Awake to the importance of a Christian life. Have supreme concern for the soul. See that it has the vestment of righteousness. Thus secure by repentance of sin, faith in the Lord Jesus, obedience to the Gospel, and thus, by timely care and preparation, the Lord of the harvest will find you ready when He comes."

After another prayer, those present took final leave of that beautiful face, and then the procession moved slowly to the churchyard. The body had found its sepulchre. In hope, we laid it away. On the morning of the resurrection, this grave will give back to us the body changed into the Christly image. For that glad day the heart longeth!

V.

" Thou feedest them with the bread of tears."—PSALM, lxxx. 5.

" Weeping may endure for a night, but joy cometh in the morning."—PSALM, xxx. 5.

" Then mourn we not beloved dead,
Ev'n while we come to weep and pray ;
The happy spirit hath but fled
To brighter realms of heavenly day :
Immortal hope dispels the gloom—
An angel sits beside the tomb."—MISS S. P. ADAMS.

She whom our souls loved, is not, for God took her.
The mind is very slow to admit the fact. But each passing
hour impresses the sad reality of absence. The pain of
separation is too constant and keen, to allow the heart for a
moment to suppose it unreal. Not as dead however, do we

mourn her, for she only sleepeth. Sweet is the thought and as balm to the bleeding heart, that she rests in the arms of Him who "giveth His beloved sleep." Nevertheless, bitter grief prevails, because she is not here. Who can stay the tears when dear ones are laid in the grave? It is no sin to weep over them. Jesus mingled his tears with those of the family of Bethany, in their bereavement. To weep is not to murmur. Tears are the outlet of sorrow. The weeping eye oft saves the breaking heart. Although tear-blinded and grief-worn, there may be only the more clearly discerned the brightness in the firmament of God's love. With riper assurance and greater steadfastness, may the heart turn to that better country, where all tears are wiped from the eyes.

The heart's great struggle is not then, to cease from weeping, but rather, while weeping, to kiss the rod that smites, and to endure the furnace with patient spirit; persuaded that One, with "form like the Son of God," is also there in loving presence.

It does not relieve the suffering spirit to attempt a concealment of any of its sorrows. The heart asks to know fully, its own bitterness. Deeply as the iron hath entered, so deeply go. As must be known the extent of the fearful malady, in order to successfully arrest its progress, so measure to the uttermost the whole height and depth of the sorrow, that to root and branch may be applied the balm of consolation. A surface view of the hurts of the spirit, only admits of partial sight of the love and power of Him who healeth. They love most who feel they have most forgiven. So do they the most rejoice in tribulation, who, "out of the depths," look up and cry unto the Father. One who fought a good fight and who did run well the race of life, has left this record of his experience: "I take pleasure in infirmities, in reproaches, in necessities, in persecutions, in distresses for Christ's sake; for when I am weak, then am I strong." Another has cheered the sufferer in sweet words of song, as if the loving Saviour Himself did speak.

> Thou plainest in thy deepest woe
> Shalt feel me at thy side;
> And, for my praise, to all shalt show
> Thou art well satisfied.

No greater sorrow befalls us than that these pages chronicle. Words utterly fail to tell it. In the language of the tear and sigh it is conveyed, and in the deepest places of the soul is it registered, far withdrawn from human gaze. The grief hardest to bear is in these secret places, whither no sympathy can reach.

Such is thy grief, brother, whose heart has been rent, and from whom part of very self has been taken. Buried from thy sight, but not lost! No less thine because invisible! Hers now, is a spirit moving in the higher sphere of pure and holy experience. Even while with thee in this realm so gross, was she lifted by the genuine impulse of holy affection to this high place. The disposition, the thought, the emotion, were reflected by the outward walk. When removed, she passed from view like a setting sun, that leaves

"A track of glory in the skies."

Mourn not the blessed translation. Not long hence, the intervening veil will be rent from top to bottom; the most excellent glory will appear; and, robed in the attire of Heaven, thine own again shall be with thee. Out of this mystery of grief will yet come a more perfect union of hearts, a consummated bliss. Thy children—whose wants unmet in later years, whose heart-yearnings after a mother's love, caress, tender care, none can measure—with thee, may go to that ransomed spirit. The broken household may be one again. Through Him who heals the ruptured brotherhood of man, and effects a "restitution of all things," who makes Mercy and Grace superabound where sin has ravaged, and who extinguishes the work and power of Death, shall all who trust in and partake of the Divine Name be exalted, re-united, perfected in holiness, and introduced to a life that shall be an endless canticle of praise.

And you who gave her birth—your hearts are stored with precious memories. He who gave hast taken, and you can bless the Name of the Lord. Promises, rich and comforting, are proffered. The realm that lies forward invites you to an infinite compensation for every sorrow here. The sacrifice is only for the present. Hereafter, she whom thou dost surrender will be eternally radiant with the light of Heaven. Rest then in hope. Not long wilt thou tarry here. The pilgrimage is nearly closed. The door of Heaven even now opens— enter in.

Thee, now only left to stay and cheer declining days, this sundered tie leaves in speechless grief. Lone and drear, a brother's heart! But that sister's pure spirit is still with thee. Death not always occasions separation. The spirit still embodied sees not the disembodied; but the invisible is no less real than the visible. Hearts bound together by loving sympathy, never lose the sense of a common presence. Where oneness is, a sense of absence cannot prevail. When time and space interpose, hearts are not drawn into isolation. The union of loving, sympathetic souls is perpetual. Death takes from the sight, not from the heart.

Of those natures that impress by their nobleness, Goethe has affirmed as a prerogative, "that their departure to higher regions exercises a no less blessed influence than did their abode on earth; that they lighten us from above like stars, by which to steer our course, often interrupted by storms." A new star has been set for thee, whose serene ray now falls as a presiding light upon thy path. The remembrance of her in the new sphere hath charms that were not when clothed in clay. The voice as it lingers in the chambers of memory is sweeter than song. The whole life so pure and good in thine eyes, abides now with thee as a mellowing leaven. Whilst thou dost mourn that a lamp has gone out on earth, yet flows there not over the soul a tide of joy because a brighter light is set above?

V I.

"The memory of the just is blessed."—Proverbs, x. 7.

"Their works do follow them."—Rev., xiv. 13.

"Such be my rest! I ask no shew
  To gild the dark vale's gloom;
Nor golden pageantry to strew
  A pathway to the tomb:
But one fond tear from those I love,
  As dust to dust is given:
And one bright flower to bloom above,
  And note my hope of Heaven."—Latrobe.

The tear has fallen over thy precious dust, and as oft as spring-time comes, and the soft sunshine and the warm dews fall upon the earth, shall the flower above thy grave bloom as thine own fond emblem, and scatter its fragrance as thine own dear name sheds its perfume in the circle of thine earthly love.

Friends have come from far to bring tributes of affection. They delight to linger around thy tomb. With tender finger, they weave the pure white garland and hang it on thy head-stone. They trace too with pen, moved by the inspiration of love, memorial-words that will never let thee die out of the memory.

He who now writes, but poorly tells the tale of thy life, yet with heart in true response to the life he here records. The character, so open to the light, he can no more trace in words than can the beauty and glory of the sunbeam be writ-ten. But when the poverty of language forbids a just record, God opens upon the world a stream of influence, upon whose every wave and ripple glistens the name. And thus thou shalt live when these pages molder and are lost.

To what has now been said of the excellency of this dear friend, will be added contributions from those who knew her long and well. They are admitted precisely as given by the respective authors.

The Pitcher of Tears.

BY PETER STRYKER, D.D.

There is a beautiful German legend to this effect:

A mother loved her child so intensely that she could not bear to be separated from her. At length the beloved one grew sick. For three days and nights the fond mother wept as well as watched and prayed, and then her darling died. A nameless sorrow seized her heart. She was alone on God's earth. Her weeping continued day and night. At length, full of sadness and weary with her tears, as she sat where the dear one died, the door gently opened, and lo! her child stood before her. She was a happy angel, beautiful as one trans-figured, and smiled sweetly in her innocence. In her hand she bore a pitcher, full to the brim.

"Mother," said the child, "weep no more. For see, this pitcher holds the tears which thou hast shed, and which the angel of grief has gathered therein. And if thou dost shed but another tear, then must the pitcher overflow, and I shall no longer have peace in my grave and joy in heaven. There-fore, O mother! weep no more, for thy child is well above, is happy, and has angels for her mates."

"And," concludes the story, "so strong and mighty is a mother's love, that she stilled her soul's deep pain, and wept no other tear."

I am reminded of this old legend on hearing of the late death of a well-remembered and beloved former parishioner.

Looking into the past with mental vision, I distinctly see a fair young girl, just budding into womanhood. Well may father, mother and brother love her devotedly, and friends hail her approach with admiration. There is something in her appearance which attracts the notice and engages the interest even of strangers. But what is it that gives a beautiful thoughtfulness to that cheerful face? And what is it that tempers that youthful sprightliness, and mingles sobriety with joy? It is piety, heaven-born piety. That maiden, like Mary, loves to sit at Jesus' feet, and with her lustrous eye look up into His face, with her attentive ear listen to His voice, with her soul full of contrition and love, receive His benediction In process of time, she gives her name with her heart to the Saviour, and, united with His disciples, begins a holy and consistent life. She is no uncertain Christian, but an "epistle known and read of all men," which gives its testimony in favor of truth and righteousness.

Another union soon occurs. We see our friend in queenly beauty at her lovely home. She is arrayed in bridal attire, and standing among a throng of loving and beloved ones at Hymen's altar; she receives the ring in pledge of love that promises to be bright, pure, and unending, and, in return, she gives her heart and hand to one who proves himself worthy of her womanly confidence and affection.

Years pass away, and Elizabeth Platt, the wife of Charles H. Adams, beloved and lamented by all who knew her, sleeps in Jesus. Little Sara lies by her side, and Mary and Willie, the oldest and youngest born, remain to mingle their tears with their father's at their mother's grave.

"Jesus wept," and so may you, dear friends; and, according to the prayer of David, God will put your tears in His bottle. But you must not weep immoderately. Let not the pitcher, already full, overflow with rebellious tears. She whose premature death you deplore is, without doubt, with the angels in heaven. Her weary journey is ended. Her life here of toil and care, of sickness and mortality, is completed, and she is now forever at rest and in bliss. She will not be saddened by your grief—she is beyond such influences—or come to chide your excessive sorrow. But God will be displeased if you murmur at his Providence, and your hearts will be injured by the overflow of the pitcher of tears.

Peace, troubled souls! Trust in the Saviour she loved so well—to whom she gave her youthful heart; who was her chief joy in health, her support in sickness, her hope in death, and is now her best beloved Friend and Companion in heaven.

He will comfort and cheer your stricken hearts.   And if the cherished object of your affection may not come back to you in angel form, you will at last go to meet her where all tears will be wiped away.   O how transporting the thought!   To enter the heavenly mansions; to see Jesus upon His throne; to wear the crown and diadem of the redeemed; to hear the anthem of angels; to join the choir that sings in sweetest strains redemption's song; to behold eternal sunshine; to eat and drink abundantly; to glide along on a calm sea that never has a ripple on its waves; to sing with millions, and not one note of discord; and all the while the voice becoming attuned to higher and sweeter notes, the ear to drink in more delicious melodies, the mind expanding to comprehend richer truths, and the heart developing to the experience and expression of purer and fuller love—O this is heaven and heaven's bliss! And there ye, who bend in sorrow at the tomb of this beloved one, if ye trust in Jesus, ye shall meet her and each other, to renew the sweet intercourse began on earth, but which in heaven will never end.

And that this may be the experience of you all, is the sincere and fervent prayer of one who cherishes in sweet recollection the period, now more than a decade in the past, when some of you, with her whose loss you mourn, were wont to call him by the endearing name of *pastor*.

Reflections on the Death of Mrs. Elizabeth Adams.

BY A FORMER PASTOR, PETER STRYKER, D.D., WHO RECEIVED HER TO CHURCH MEMBERSHIP, OFFICIATED AT HER MARRIAGE, AND REMEMBERS WITH JOY HER LOVELY PIETY.

I.

Thy sun has set; but still the golden hue

   Of twilight sky delights our thoughtful gaze;

For though thou art forever borne from view,

   Thy mem'ry lives to light the evening haze:

A beam of light comes streaming from thy tomb,

And sheds a mellow radiance 'mid the gloom.

II.

Thy sun has set; but not a single cloud

   Hangs in the Western sky;—all is serene.

No doubts and fears thy destiny enshroud,

    To cast their shadows o'er the tranquil scene.

Thy toil is o'er, thy weary race is run,

Life's battles fought, the final victory won.

III.

Thy sun is set; but one bright, twinkling star

    Grows more effulgent in the evening sky;

Bright orb of hope, it sweetly shines from far

    And sends its rays of joy and comfort nigh.

That star o'er Judah's plains its lustre shed,

And still it shines o'er all the pious dead.

IV.

Thy sun has set, but once again will rise

    When the long night of ages shall be past;

Nay, even now, through other, brighter skies,

The gentle rays of holy love are cast,

And thou, departed one! a Christian here,

Art now, we know, an orb in yonder sphere.

V.

Then shall we mourn thy sun has early set?

No, though we walk 'mid gloomy shades of night,

We'll trust in Jesus, and will ne'er forget

The day will dawn, the day surpassing bright,

Then husband, children, parents, brother, friend,

A blest eternity with thee we'll spend.

In Memory of Mrs. Adams.

Away, away to the mansions of light—

Our well-beloved hath taken her flight!

Away from sorrow, away from pain,

No dark valley to trouble again!

Ransomed from death by her Saviour in love,

Now basking in joy, she liveth above.

Eyes of rare beauty, lips of true love,

Smile like a sunbeam from gardens above;

Voice like an angel's, silvery sweet,

Thrilling like music our souls to entreat—

Purer and brighter and lovelier far,

She now shines in heaven, a glorious star.

Free from temptation, free from all sin,

With no more victories o'er each to win;

In robes pure and white our darling appears,

While sweet songs of welcome are greeting her ears.

A new name in heaven is known from this day,

A new crown given that ne'er shall decay.

Though far from our sight her spirit hath flown,

Where farewells and tears shall never be known;

Her sweet heart's love will think of us there,

Listening with joy for each word of prayer;

Then, wafting it on to her Saviour's white throne,

He'll plead for her friends, her kindred and home.

Thou beautiful vision! passing away

Like foretaste of heaven athwart our dark way!

Though God gave, He but lent thee; He did recall,

And while our hearts grieve thee, so dear to us all,

We fain would remember that God reigns above,

And though He afflicts us, 'tis always in love.

E. H.

Saratoga Springs, Oct. 5th, 1866.

Lines in Memory of Mrs. Elizabeth Platt Adams.

Dear, sainted friend! imprinted on my heart,

Thy spiritual features, sweet and fair,

In colors fadeless, thence will ne'er depart

While memory lasts, and life is active here.

Swiftly have sped the few revolving years

Since thou, a timid stranger, and a bride

In youthful beauty, between hopes and fears,

First came, to find among us friends untried.

Soon, all loved who knew thee—best knew, loved most:

Thy prospects all were bright—none saw the cloud

Of sad bereavements, like a full-clad host,

That hovered o'er, thy happiness to shroud:

But all too soon to sable weeds of woe,

Changing the bridal robes, it swooping fell,

When one, thou hadst but just begun to know

And love as sister, in new ties, full well,

A bride of one short year, was called away.

Again, and yet again, with cruel hand,

Did death, the dark-browed monarch, wield his sway,

Till few were left of all the loving band

Who welcomed thee as daughter, sister dear.

What wonder that thy pensive features took

A sadder cast, that in thine eye a tear

Oft mingled with each tender, loving look.

But *now*, thy tears are changed to smiles of joy ;

Thou canst not weep with those *now* left in woe,

Who, while they mourn, rejoice that no alloy

79

Thy happiness in Heaven e'er can know.

Sweet daughter, sister, mother, wife, and friend,

Again we hope to meet thee when is run

Our earthly race—when time with us shall end,

And our eternal, blissful life's begun.

E. M. BECKER.

COHOES, Dec. 28th, 1866.

The extracts that follow are from a fugitive piece of one of the sweetest bards of this country. They are incorporated here, because the lines so fitly express fact and sentiment connected with the sickness and death of Mrs. Adams. Selected by him who has a bitter experience of all narrated, they will be read with lively interest and deep emotion:

Yes, dear one, I am dying.   Hope at times

Has whispered to me in her syren tones,

But now, alas! I feel the tide of life

Fast ebbing from my heart.   I know that soon

The green and flowery curtain of the grave

Will close as softly round my fading form

As the calm shadows of the evening hour

Close o'er the fading stream.

                                        Oh! there are times

When my heart's tears gush wildly at the thought

I must resign my breath.   To me the earth

Is very beautiful.   I love its flowers,

Its birds, its dews, its rainbows, its glad streams,

Its vales, its mountains, its green, wooing woods,

Its moonlight clouds, its sunsets, and its soft

And dewy twilights; and I needs must mourn

To think that I shall pass away,

And see them nevermore.

                     But thou, the loved

And fondly cherished idol of my life,

Thou dear twin-spirit of my deathless soul,

'Twill be the keenest anguish of my heart

To part from thee.　True, we have never loved

With the wild passion that fills heart and brain

With flame and madness, yet my love for thee

Is my life's life.　A deeper, holier love

Has never sighed and wept beneath the stars,

Or glowed within the breasts of saints in heaven.

It does not seem a passion of my heart;

It is a portion of my soul.　I feel

That I am but a softened shade of thee,

And that my spirit, parted from thine own,

Might fade and perish from the universe

Like a star-shadow when the star itself

Is hidden by the storm-cloud.   Ay, I fear

That heaven itself, though filled with love and God,

Will be to me all desolate, if thou,

Dear spirit, art not there.   I've often prayed

That I might die before thee, for I felt

I could not dwell without thee on the earth,

And now my heart is breaking at the thought

Of dying while thou livest, for I feel,

My life's dear idol, that I cannot dwell

Without thee in the sky.   Yet well I know

That love like ours, so holy, pure and high,

So far above the passions of the earth,

Can perish not with mortal life.   In heaven

'Twill brighten to a lovely star, and glow

In the far ages of eternity,

More beautiful and radiant than when first

'Twas kindled into glory.   Oh! I love,

I dearly love thee—these will be my last,

My dying words upon the earth, and they

Will be my first when we shall meet in heaven;

And when ten thousand myriads of years

Shall fade into the past eternity,

My soul will breathe the same dear words to thine,

I love thee, oh! I love thee!

                                        Weak and low

My pulse of life is fluttering at my heart,

84

And soon 'twill cease forever.   These faint words

Are the last echoes of the spirit's chords,

Stirred by the breath of memory.

    *   * * * * *

         And, dear one, now

I feel that my poor heart must bid farewell

To thine.   Oh! no, no, dearest! not farewell,

For oft I will be with thee on the earth,

Although my home be heaven.   At eventide,

When thou art wandering by the silent stream,

To muse upon the sweet and mournful past,

I will walk with thee, hand in hand, and share

Thy gentle thoughts and fancies; in thy grief,

When all seems dark and desolate around

Thy bleak and lonely pathway, I will glide

Like a bright shadow o'er thy soul, and charm

Away thy sorrow; in the quiet hush

Of the deep night, when thy dear head is laid

Upon thy pillow, and thy spirit craves

Communion with my spirit, I will come

To nerve thy heart with strength, and gently lay

My lips upon thy forehead, with a touch

Like the soft kisses of the southern breeze

Stealing o'er bowers of roses; when the wild,

Dark storms of life beat fiercely on thy head,

Thou wilt behold my semblance on the cloud,

A rainbow to thy spirit; I will bend

At times above the fount within thy soul,

And thou wilt see my image in its depths,

Gazing into thy dark eyes with a smile

As I gazed in life.   And I will come   ,

To thee in dreams, my spirit-mate, and we,

With clasping hands and intertwining wings,

Will nightly wander o'er the starry deep,

And by the blessed streams of Paradise,

Loving in heaven as we have loved on earth.